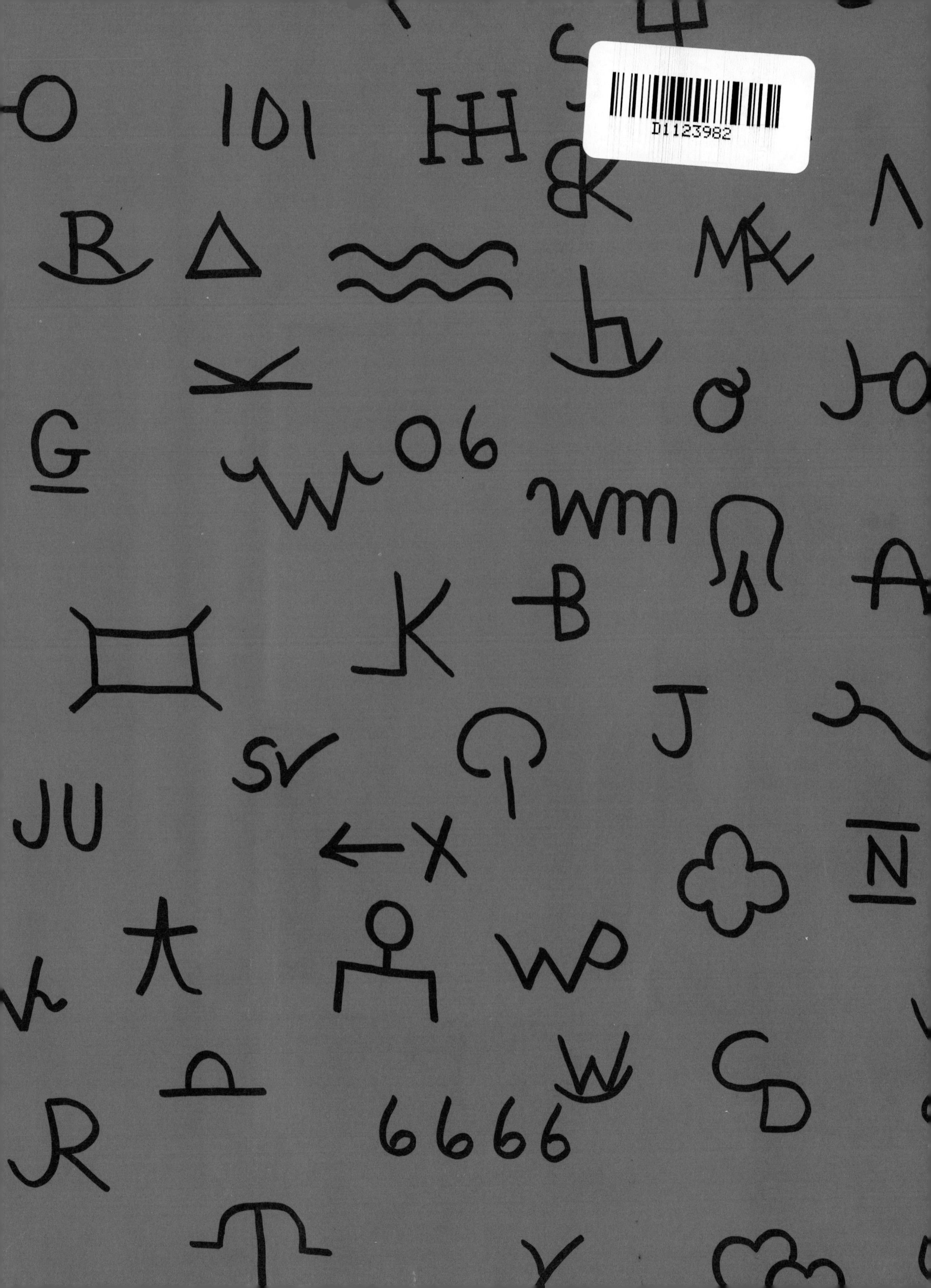

DATE DUE

MAY 25 2000	JUL 30 2003		
JUN 10 2000	FEB 21 2004		
AUG 28 2000	APR 10 2004		
AUG 31 2000	APR 31 2004		
SEP 11 2000			
OCT 01 2000	MAY 21 2004		
SEP 02 2001	SEP 19 2004		
JUN 29 2002	APR 28 2006		
AUG 12 2002	MAY 25 2006		
OCT 25 2002	SEP 18 2006		
FEB 15 2003	OCT 21 2006		
MAY 24 2003	MY 10 08		

WHY COWBOYS NEED A BRAND

WHY COWBOYS NEED A BRAND

By Laurie Lazzaro Knowlton
Illustrated by James Rice

PELICAN PUBLISHING COMPANY
Gretna 1996

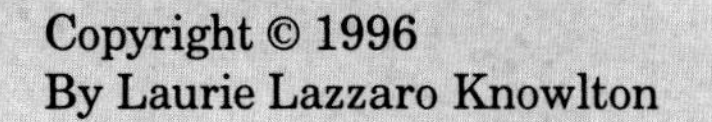

In the beginning there was the Word (John 1:1)

To my Creator
and all those who believed in me—
thank you

Library of Congress Cataloging-in-Publication Data

Knowlton, Laurie Lazzaro.
Why cowboys need a brand / by Laurie Lazzaro Knowlton ;
illustrated by James Rice.
p. cm.
Summary: Cowboy Slim Jim Watkins has everything he needs to start his own ranch—except a unique brand.
ISBN 1-56554-228-2 (hc: alk. paper)
[1. Cowboys—Fiction. 2. Ranch life—Fiction. 3. Cattle brands--Fiction.] I. Rice, James, 1934- ill. II. Title.
PZ7.K7685We 1996
[E]—dc20 96-13713
CIP
AC

Manufactured in Singapore

Published by Pelican Publishing Company, Inc.
1101 Monroe Street, Gretna, Louisiana 70053

Why Cowboys Need a Brand

Slim Jim Watkins was one determined cowboy. Why, when all the other cowhands grumbled and said, "Nope, not me," Slim Jim Watkins would pull up on his britches and say, "Shoot, I can do that!"

A while back, the ranch foreman struck up a challenge. "You break these horses and that bangtail bronc over yonder is yours."

"Nope, not me," agreed all the cowhands. "Thar's not a man alive can break Bonecrusher."

Slim Jim Watkins hitched up his britches and said, "Shoot, I can do that!"

JMRICE

At last, Slim Jim Watkins was ready to ride Bonecrusher. He was sure his chin would drill a hole in his chest before that bangtail bronc gave up. But Slim Jim Watkins stuck to that horse like a flea on a dog.

A hush fell over the cowboys as Slim Jim Watkins slid off Bonecrusher. "Gentle as a newborn calf," he said.

The foreman handed over the reins. "A deal's a deal. A feller could start a ranch with a horse like that."

Slim Jim Watkins sighed. "A feller needs a brand if'n he's a-hankerin' for a ranch of his own."

The foreman nodded. "Can't prove an animal's your'n without a brand."

"I'll ponder on a brand while I get Bonecrusher shod," said Slim Jim Watkins.

OAT
JMRice

The very next day, the ramrod woke the cowhands. "Boys, we got a blue norther headed this way. I can feel it in my bones. Someone's gotta go round up those dogies."

All the cowhands looked at the ground. "Take on a blue norther? Nope, not me."

Well, all that talk didn't mind Slim Jim Watkins much. He just pulled up on his britches and said, "Shoot, I can do that."

JMRICE

JMRICE

The sleet whipped around Slim Jim Watkins. Sometimes he felt like he was searching for a fresh-laid egg in a snowdrift. But he rode long past saddle sore. Slim Jim Watkins rounded up all those dogies and brought them home.

"Slim!" the ramrod exclaimed. "I knew you was tougher than a wild bull!" With a slap on the back, he gave Slim Jim Watkins a dozen Longhorn.

All the cowhands gathered around. "Hey, Slim. You've got a horse and some cattle. When ya gonna head off on your own?"

"Can't do that," said Slim Jim Watkins.

"*Can't?* Did Slim Jim Watkins say *can't?*" asked a surprised cowhand.

"Can't have a ranch without a brand."

"How 'bout an *SJW* brand?" asked a cowhand.

"Can't! Been done," replied Slim Jim Watkins.

"Nope, can't have a brand that's been done," agreed all the cowhands.

That very afternoon, when the weather cleared, a snake struck at Cookie's mules.

"It's a runaway chuck wagon!" shouted one cowhand. "We've gotta catch it!"

"Can't catch it! Nobody can catch up with a chuck wagon gone wild," said the others.

"Nope, we won't be eating tonight," they all agreed.

All but Slim Jim Watkins. He spied the dust-flying commotion. "Shoot, I can do that!" he said. So he and Bonecrusher hightailed it across the range . . .

and stopped the runaway chuck wagon.

When the trail drive found the chuck wagon, Cookie was bandaged and sleeping. Biscuits were baking and Slim Jim Watkins was putting the last tin in place.

Finally Cookie dragged himself out of his wagon. He looked sorrier than a drenched cat. "Slim, my wagon's everything to me, and just to set things straight, I'm gonna hand over my deed to a little spread 'round San Antone way. Now you got all the makin's of your own ranch."

DEED

Slim Jim Watkins felt lower than a snake's belly. "I can't do that," he said. "Pretty sad situation when a feller *can* break a dozen horses, *can* round up a thousand Longhorn, *can* feed a hungry brood o' cowhands, but can't use the imagination the good Lord gave him to come up with a brand."

All the cowhands looked confounded.

Bonecrusher pawed the ground impatiently. For a moment the setting sun glittered off his horseshoe.

Slim Jim Watkins' eyes lit up like a starry Texas night. "Shoot, on second thought, I *can* do that. Yep. *Can do!*" And he did.

JMRICE